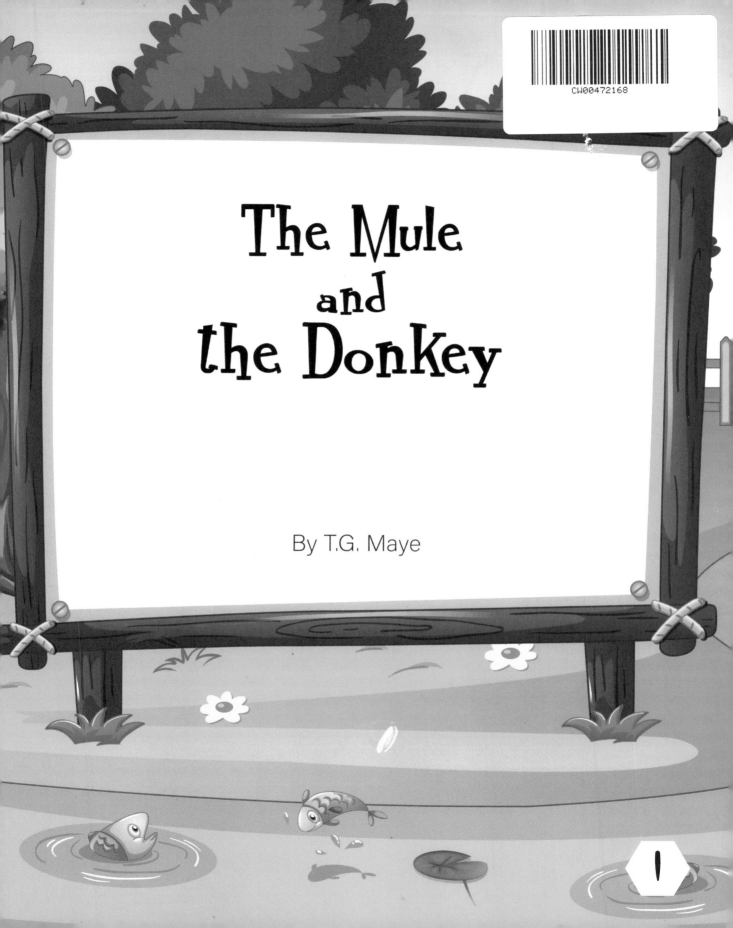

The Mule
and
the Donkey

By T.G. Maye

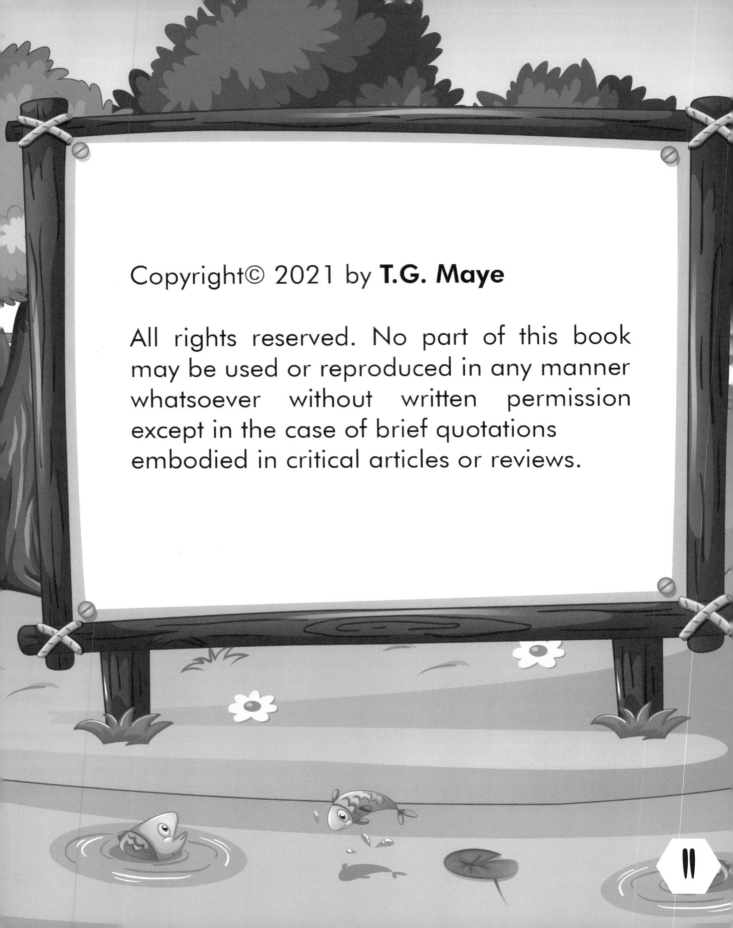

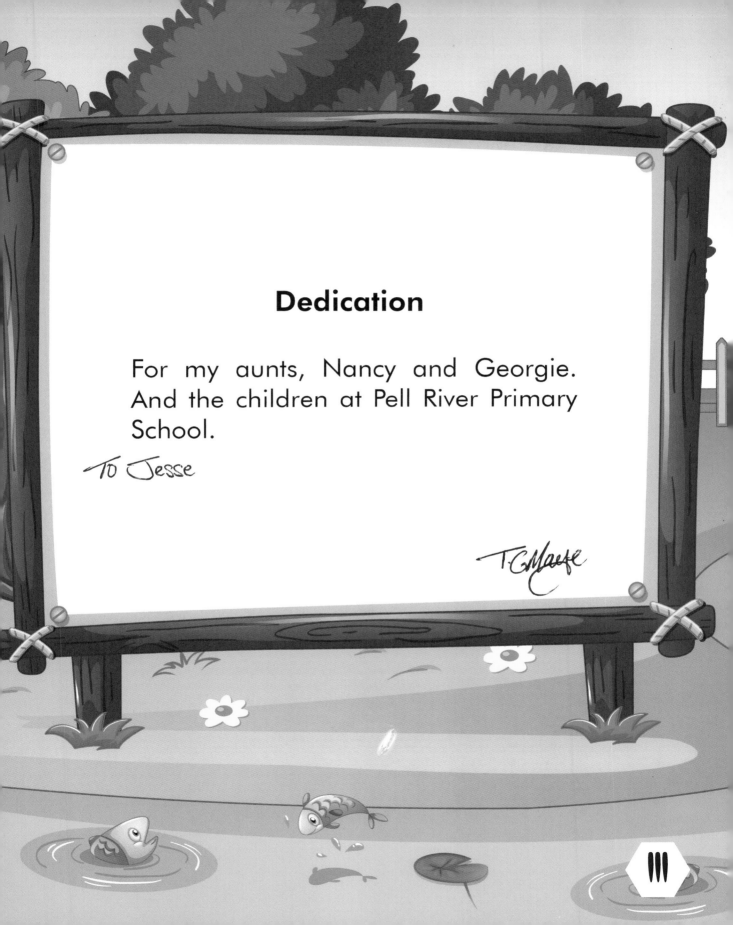

Dedication

For my aunts, Nancy and Georgie. And the children at Pell River Primary School.

To Jesse

T.G.Maafe

ILLUSTRATOR

I am Anna Scott, a Graphic Designer based in Italy. My specialised areas are in watercolour and digital illustrations.

I have illustrated over a thousand books for clients worldwide. However, that is just a glimpse into what I do. Designing is my passion, and it brings colour to my world. I spend hours working at night and arise brimming with excitement to continue at daybreak.

As a creative, the process begins with my ability to grasp the core concepts of the story. I observe and feel the character's emotions, which they want to convey.

My mission is to create art, which exceeds the author's expectations. I achieve this by drawing from a child's perspective; whilst ensuring market requirements and standards are maintained.

If you have a project and you need advice, assistance and solutions. Feel free to contact me, as I can help make your story the best it can be.

Email: **hire4solution@gmail.com**

IV

Acknowledgements

At the beginning of this journey, I knew I'd be traversing unfamiliar streets. Although the words are mine, this project is a testament to those who assisted me along the way.

I owe an irredeemable debt to Anna Scott, my guide and illustrator. Likewise, my brilliant editor, Erica M Peter, this book would never be the same without you two.

Special thanks to my wife, Beverly, for the countless hours of support and encouragement. And to Margie, Myrna and Mrs Delisser who believed when I had moments of doubt.

Finally, to my amazing colleagues at North Middlesex University Hospital, your love, time and feedback brought wind to my sails.

Timbo the donkey and his cousin, Wilmutt, the mule, live on a farm with an elderly farmer. After several years, their amiable companion passes away.

1

Facing a daunting future, the anxious animals lament his passing. However, he leaves them as the sole beneficiaries of his will, fearing his only son has died in a distant war.

One arid afternoon, the pair retreats to the shade of a large tree.

"Since our friend is no longer around, we should share the property," said Wilmutt. "This isn't necessary. There is plenty of land for the both of us," Timbo replied.

Wilmutt insists, and they converse upon the matter as relatives are supposed to do. However, the conniving creature promptly disagrees with each solution Timbo offers.

They argue until the azure sky turns orange-red. But fail to reach an agreement.

The endless bickering frustrates Timbo.
"Since you are older, I'll let you decide," he said.

"My humble cousin, I will not take advantage of you,"
said Wilmutt. "Therefore, I'll take the dangerous
section near the river. Although, it means my land will
suffer regular flooding. And I'll walk further to reach
our barn in the evenings."

7

Timbo knows Wilmutt is after the best grass, which grows along the riverbank. Furthermore, the mule will have easy access to the water holes. Yet to honour his decision, he agrees.

8

However, creating the boundary leads to another round of bickering. Once again, Wilmutt takes issue with Timbo's suggestions; yet he provides no alternatives.

They argue until the moon and stars
grow dim at the break of dawn.
Eventually, they agree to use a ball of
yarn to create the boundary.

The following day, Timbo approaches the border whilst Wilmutt is surveying his holdings. "Good day, cousin. May I pass for a drink at the waterhole?" said Timbo.

NO!!!

"Oh no, you can't! This is my land," said Wilmutt. "Go away, and find a different stream."

"Please, my throat is so dry that I fear this thirst could be the end of me," said Timbo.

His desperate plea falls on stubborn ears as Wilmutt refuses to change his stance.

"I hope his thirst gets the better of him, then I will have all the land," thinks Wilmutt.

Weary and thirsty, Timbo walks away. He trudges several miles with a pair of birds in tow; until he discovers a tiny stream.

A week later, Wilmutt wanders near the border. He stares in wonder at the lush grass on the other side and grows green with envy.

"How can it be?" said Wilmutt. "I took the area along the river-bank, yet Timbos grass is more appealing. I shall find a way to get it for myself."

That night, he sneaks over the line. But Timbo is awake and chases him back across the border.

15

The crafty Wilmutt waits for the moon to disappear behind a blanket of clouds. Then he shifts the yarn several meters inside the donkey's territory.

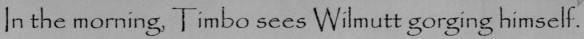

In the morning, Timbo sees Wilmutt gorging himself.
"Why are you eating my grass?" he said.
"How is it yours if it's on my side of the line?" said
Wilmutt between mouthfuls of juicy grass.

Unable to prove he owns the grass, a sullen Timbo let it be. This pattern continues until Timbo has a tiny portion of the farmland remaining.

In his greedy pursuit of Timbo's territory, Wilmutt neglects a section of his land. Eventually, a forest grows upon it. And a vicious creature makes its home in the undergrowth.

19

One sweltering and windless afternoon, Wilmutt embarks for the waterhole. After a brief trot, he enters the dim-lit forest.
Suddenly, the beast utters a mighty roar, springs from the bushes and gives chase.

The panic-stricken Wilmutt runs like the wind, screaming for Timbo to come to his aid. But the ass is miles away at the other stream. So he gallops until his tongue is hanging loose and his legs are aching.

After a lengthy chase, the beast catches Wilmutt. It quickly devours him and then returns to its lair deep in the woods.

A week later, the farmer's son returns. His beautiful wife, their adorable children, and a shaggy dog accompany him.

He slays the beast; and cuts down the forest.
Then he uses the wood to build a house and
paints it bright blue and cream.

Finally, he gives Timbo freedom to go wherever he pleases. And they all live together, happily ever after.

Printed in Great Britain
by Amazon